Lady and the Tramp

Narinder Dhami

PUFFIN BOOKS

Lady and the Tramp

PUFFIN BOOKS

Published by the Penguin Group
Penguin Books Ltd, 80 Strand, London WC2R 0RL, England
Penguin Putnam Inc., 375 Hudson Street, New York, New York 10014, USA
Penguin Books Australia Ltd, 250 Camberwell Road, Camberwell, Victoria 3124, Australia
Penguin Books Canada Ltd, 10 Alcorn Avenue, Toronto, Ontario, Canada M4V 3B2
Penguin Books India (P) Ltd, 11 Community Centre, Panchsheel Park, New Delhi – 110 017, India
Penguin Books (NZ) Ltd, Cnr Rosedale and Airborne Roads, Albany, Auckland, New Zealand
Penguin Books (South Africa) (Pty) Ltd, 24 Sturdee Avenue, Rosebank 2196, South Africa

Penguin Books Ltd, Registered Offices: 80 Strand, London WC2R 0RL, England

www.penguin.com

First published 2003
1

Set in 16/25 Cochin

Made and printed in England by Clays Ltd, St Ives plc

British Library Cataloguing in Publication Data
A CIP catalogue record for this book is available from the British Library

ISBN 0–141–31648–9

Contents

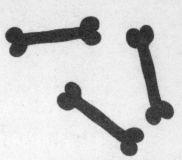

Chapter One

Lady sat in the garden with her head on her paws. Her tail wasn't wagging and her ears drooped. She didn't even notice the birds swooping down to peck at the food in the bowl beside her.

The little spaniel was feeling very miserable. Something was upsetting her and she couldn't explain it to herself. She hadn't felt this unhappy since the time before she'd come to live with Jim Dear and Darling all those months ago ...

Lady's big brown eyes lit up for a moment as she remembered the perfect Christmas when she'd arrived at her new home. It had been snowing outside and a glittering Christmas tree stood in a corner of the living room. Just a tiny puppy, Lady had sat quietly inside the big box that was wrapped in paper and adorned with ribbons. She could hear excited voices.

Suddenly the lid of the box was lifted off. Lady peeped out shyly and looked up at a smiling face.

'Oh, how sweet!' exclaimed Darling, Jim's wife. 'What a perfectly beautiful little lady!'

And that was how Lady had got her name. Right from the start, she had been very happy with Jim Dear and Darling, but that first Christmas night she had felt all alone. Jim had put the puppy in her basket in the kitchen, but Lady didn't want to be left all alone while her owners went upstairs to bed. Jumping out of her basket, she raced after them, whining.

'Oh, look,' said Darling. 'She's lonely. Maybe – just for tonight?'

'No, darling,' Jim said firmly. 'We've got to show her who's master!'

Lady's tail wagged just a little as she remembered how she had howled and whimpered and then sneaked upstairs to sleep on her owners' bed. She'd slept there ever since too. Every day she woke Jim by tugging the covers off him or bouncing up and down on the bed. Then

she would race downstairs, through the
dog door and out into the garden, where
the blackbirds sang. She would wait
there to collect the newspaper from the
paper boy, and sometimes she would
chase the big, fat black rat that lived in
the woodpile.

Lady lifted her head and growled as
she stared at the woodpile over in the
corner of the garden. The rat never came
when Lady was around, but she knew he
was there all right.

'That old rat had better watch out,'
Lady told herself. She was getting bigger
every day. Why, just a week or two ago
she'd turned six months old. Jim Dear
and Darling had bought her a dog licence
and a brand-new blue collar. Lady was

very proud of her collar. She thought back to how she'd shown it off to Jock and Trusty, the two dogs who were her best friends ...

'Well, lassie, that's a bonnie new collar,' Jock barked when he saw it. 'It must be very expensive.'

Lady tossed her head with pleasure.

'Let's go and show it to Trusty,' the Scottie said.

So they trotted down the street towards Trusty's house. They found the bloodhound fast asleep on the front porch, snoring loudly. His nose twitched as a caterpillar landed on it.

'He's dreaming,' said Lady, laughing.

'Aye,' Jock agreed, 'dreaming of those

days when he and his grandfather used to track criminals through the swamps. But that was before –' he lowered his voice – 'before he lost his sense of smell.'

'Oh no!' Lady gasped.

'But we must never let on that we know, lassie,' Jock insisted. 'It would break his heart.'

Trusty was sniffing at the caterpillar, who slid off the dog's nose and disappeared into an nearby hole. 'Which way did he go?' Trusty barked. Then, seeing Lady and Jock, he came over. 'He was a big fellow, about six foot two. Wore a striped suit.'

Jock glanced at Lady, as if to say, 'You see?'

'Why, Miss Lady, you have a collar,'

Trusty barked, beaming at her. 'My, my, how time flies.'

'Aye, it seems like only yesterday she was cutting her teeth on Jim Dear's slippers,' agreed Jock.

'Oh, look! It's Jim Dear,' Lady barked as she saw her master coming up the street. 'He's home from work. Please excuse me.' And with that she dashed off to greet him.

They arrived home together to see Darling waiting for them at the front door, and then all three of them settled down for one of the cosy, quiet evenings that Lady loved so much.

'With Lady here, I'd say that life is quite complete,' Jim Dear announced, as they sat in front of the fire.

'Yes, dear,' replied Darling. 'I don't imagine anything could ever take her place in our hearts.'

Lady had felt very happy and very loved then, sitting there in her new collar, but now everything had changed.

Chapter Two

Jock and Trusty trotted through the gate of Lady's house and looked around the front garden.

'Lassie!' Jock called. 'Are you here?'

'Miss Lady!' Trusty woofed.

They made their way to the corner of the house and peered into the back garden. Lady was there, slumped on the ground by her food bowl, looking very unhappy.

'Ah, good morning, lassie,' barked

Jock. ''Tis a bonnie bright day –' He stopped as he suddenly realized how miserable Lady looked.

'Why, Miss Lady,' Trusty exclaimed. 'Is something wrong?'

Jock sat down to scratch himself. 'Aye, tell us, lassie. If somebody's been mistreating you –'

'Oh no, Jock.' Lady looked puzzled. 'It's something I've done, I guess.'

Trusty was taken aback. 'You?'

'It must be,' Lady replied sadly.

'Now, lassie, get on with the details,' Jock told her.

'Well, I first noticed it the other day,' Lady began. 'When Jim Dear came home and I went to meet him.'

Lady told Jock and Trusty how she

had rushed out of the front door as Jim arrived home. She'd jumped up to say hello, but he'd gone right past her and straight into the house, calling, 'Darling! Are you all right?'

'Of course I am.' Darling smiled, as Lady looked on, feeling very puzzled. 'Why shouldn't I be?'

'I just can't help worrying,' Jim had replied. 'Alone here all day in your condition and walking that dog.'

'THAT DOG!' Jock and Trusty barked, their eyes round.

Lady's head drooped. 'He's never called me that before.'

'Now, lassie, don't worry your wee head about it,' Jock replied. 'Remember, they're only humans after all.'

'And then there's Darling,' Lady went on. 'We've always enjoyed our walk together every afternoon. But yesterday, when I ran into the living room carrying my lead ...'

Lady's eyes grew dark and sad as she remembered how Darling had shaken her head. 'No, Lady,' she had said, while sitting on the sofa and knitting a pair of bootees. 'No walk today.' Lady had been so disappointed that she'd grabbed the ball of wool and run off with it. That had made Darling cross and she'd slapped Lady on the bottom.

'It didn't hurt,' Lady sighed, staring mournfully up at Jock and Trusty. 'But Darling has never hit me before ...'

Jock and Trusty looked at each other.

'Now, lassie, don't take it too seriously.' Jock smiled.

Trusty cleared his throat. 'Yes, you see, Miss Lady,' he woofed, 'there comes a time in the life of all humans when – er – the birds and the bees, you know?'

Lady looked puzzled.

'What he's trying to say, lassie,' Jock cut in, 'is that Darling is expecting a wee bairn.'

Lady looked even more puzzled. 'Bairn?'

'He means a baby, Miss Lady,' Trusty explained.

'OH!' Lady nodded her head with a smile. 'Er – what's a baby?'

'Well, they look like humans,' Jock said wisely.

'But a mite smaller,' Trusty added.

'Aye,' Jock went on, 'and they walk on all fours.'

'And if I remember correctly –' Trusty frowned – 'they bellow a lot.'

'They're very expensive,' said Jock. 'And you're not allowed to play with them.'

'But they're mighty sweet,' Trusty finished off.

'Just a cute little bundle,' another voice cut in. 'Ha ha ha!'

Chapter Three

Lady, Jock and Trusty looked round in surprise. A big, grey, battered-looking dog with cheeky dark eyes was standing at the gate.

'Just a cute bundle of trouble,' the dog went on. He trotted across the garden towards them. 'Home wreckers, that's what they are.'

'Look here, laddie.' Jock began to bristle. 'Who are you to barge in and –'

'My name's Tramp and I'm the voice of

experience!' the dog broke in. He turned to Lady. 'Just you wait till Junior gets here,' he warned her. 'You get the urge for a nice comfortable scratch and next thing you know it's: "Put that dog out or it'll get fleas all over the baby!" You start barking at some strange mutt: "Stop that racket! You'll wake the baby!"' He glanced over his shoulder. 'You end up living on the streets and trying to escape from the dog catcher – like me.'

Lady was beginning to look very worried.

'Don't listen, lassie,' Jock barked quickly. 'No human is that cruel.'

'Why, everybody knows a dog's best friend is his human,' Trusty agreed.

Tramp burst out laughing. 'Oh, come

on, fellas,' he said, smiling, 'you haven't fallen for that old line, have you?'

Jock glared at him. 'We've no need for mongrels and their strange ideas here,' he snapped. 'Off with you now!'

'OK, OK.' Tramp backed away slowly, looking at Lady. 'But just remember, pigeon – when a baby moves in, the dog moves out!'

Lady had thought about Tramp's words many times over the months that followed. Although Jim Dear and Darling were never unkind to her, they were thinking about the baby much more than about their little dog.

Then came the stormy, rainy night in April when the baby was finally born.

Lady sat and watched everything going on around her as the doctor arrived and spent a long time up in the bedroom with Darling. Eventually, Jim dashed downstairs, looking very excited, and grabbed the telephone.

'Aunt Sarah?' he gabbled. 'It's a boy! It's a boy!'

'But what is a baby?' Lady asked herself. She decided that it must be something wonderful, because everyone looked so excited.

Lady didn't get to see the baby until a few days later. Then she sneaked upstairs and into the bedroom. Jim Dear was downstairs making a bottle and Darling was putting the baby to sleep. Lady padded into the room and looked over the edge of the cradle. The baby is beautiful, she thought happily. Darling gently scratched Lady's long, fluffy ears and the spaniel felt part of the family again. What on earth had that funny dog, Tramp, been talking about? Everything was going to be fine!

Chapter Four

'Oh, Jim, I just can't leave him,'
Darling said anxiously. 'He's still so small
and helpless.'

'He'll be all right,' Jim replied, picking
up the suitcase.

Lady looked angrily from Jim Dear to
Darling. Where were they going? They
couldn't leave the baby all alone. He was
only six months old! Lady felt very cross
indeed. When Jim put out a hand to
stroke her, she pulled away.

'Hey, what's the matter with Lady?'
Jim frowned.

'Oh!' Darling said. 'She thinks we're
running out on him.'

'Don't worry, Lady.' Jim squatted
down in front of her. 'We have to go
away for a few days. But Aunt Sarah's
coming to look after the baby – and you
can help her!'

Lady felt very relieved. When the
doorbell rang, she dashed downstairs to
see what Aunt Sarah was like.

'Sorry I'm late, dear.' Aunt Sarah
opened the door herself, carrying
numerous bags and baskets. She bustled
in, trapping Lady between the door and
the wall. 'Now, you two, get on your
way.' She beamed at Jim and Darling.

'Don't worry about a thing.'

Lady wriggled out from behind the door in time to see Jim and Darling wave goodbye. Then, feeling sad, she ran upstairs after Aunt Sarah, who had gone to see the baby.

'Coochie-coo,' she cooed, leaning over the cradle. Then she spotted Lady and her face darkened. 'What are you doing in here? Scat!'

Lady was shocked. As she trotted out of the room, the door slammed behind her. Feeling hurt and confused, she went downstairs. Aunt Sarah had left her luggage in the hall and Lady was surprised to see the lid of the big basket slowly opening. Two cats with slanted blue eyes stared out at her.

'We are Siamese, if you please,' they purred at her. Then they leapt lightly out of the basket and set off to explore.

Curious, Lady went after them. They were heading for the birdcage in the corner of the room until Lady barked and chased them away. Instead they jumped up on to the piano, scratching the wood and knocking a vase of flowers off it. Then they jumped on to the curtains and slid down them, shredding the material with their sharp claws. Lady watched in horror.

Upstairs the baby was crying. The cats looked at each other in delight.

'Where there's a baby, there's milk,' one of them said.

They made for the stairs, but Lady

rushed to stop them. Growling, she chased them back into the living room, where they climbed up the curtains again. Lady got tangled up in the curtains and bumped into a picture stand, which fell over with a crash.

'What's going on here?'

Aunt Sarah rushed into the room and gasped as she saw the damage. The two cats sat innocently on the floor, while Lady cowered under the curtain.

'Oh, my darlings!' Aunt Sarah swept her cats up into her arms. 'Oh, that wicked animal!'

Before Lady knew what was happening, Aunt Sarah had grabbed her roughly, snapping on her lead and marching her down to the pet shop.

'I want a muzzle,' she told the shop assistant. 'A good, strong muzzle.'

Lady was very frightened as the shop assistant put the muzzle round her head. She struggled wildly, trying to get away.

'Stop it now!' Aunt Sarah scolded, as the man tightened the straps.

But Lady was too scared to listen. Pulling herself free, she dashed to the door and ran out into the street, trailing her lead behind her.

Chapter Five

Panting with fright, Lady ran across the street. She was almost hit by a car, but it managed to brake just in time. She spotted a nearby alley and dodged down it, thinking she would be safe, but suddenly three dogs appeared from behind the dustbins. Barking loudly, they flew towards her.

Lady was terrified. She pelted down the alley, with the dogs snapping at her heels. She crossed the railway tracks,

'What a perfectly beautiful little lady!'

'Just remember, pigeon — when a baby moves in, the dog moves out!'

Lady felt part of the family again. Everything was going to be fine

Aunt Sarah gasped when she saw the damage. 'Oh, that wicked animal

Barking loudly, the three dogs snapped at Lady's heels.

'What you need is a log puller,' Tramp pointed out.

'...here's a great big hunk of world out there,' Tramp told Lady.

'If you've never chased chickens, you've never lived!' Tramp shouted

'What did you do, sweetheart?' asked Bull. 'Give the butler fleas?'

'Who's Trixie?' Lady demanded. 'And Lulu, Fifi and Rosita?'

Lady pulled back the curtain and there lay the dead rat.

'It's Jock and Trusty!' Jim called.

Life couldn't be more perfect.

trying to lose them, then turned down another alley. In minutes she had skidded to a halt. It was a dead end. Cowering in fear, Lady turned to face the three dogs, who were now close behind her.

But before they could attack, another dog appeared from the shadows. He snarled loudly and flung himself at the three dogs. Lady gasped as she recognized Tramp. She hadn't seen him for months.

The fight was fierce, but finally the other three dogs slunk away, battered and bruised. Breathing hard, Tramp turned to Lady.

'Say, pigeon, what're you doing on this side of the tracks?' he asked. Then he noticed the muzzle. 'Oh, you poor kid!

We've got to get that off right away. And I think I know the very place. Come on!'

Lady padded after Tramp as he led the way. She still felt scared, but at least now she'd found a friend.

'The zoo?' Lady said in amazement, as Tramp led her through the gates.

Tramp nodded. 'We'd better go through this place from A to Z,' he muttered. 'Alligators? No!' They walked past the monkey house. 'Apes? No!' They continued on. Suddenly Tramp stopped by a sign that read 'Beaver Dam'. A big brown beaver was chewing through a large tree branch.

'There's the answer to our problem,' Tramp said. 'Pardon me, friend,' he called.

The beaver was pushing the branch towards his dam. He stopped and looked impatiently at Tramp. 'Can't stop to gossip!'

'What you need is a log puller,' Tramp pointed out. 'And luckily you see before you the new, improved log model!' He pointed at Lady's lead and muzzle.

The beaver looked interested. 'Say, can I try it out?'

'Sure.' Tramp nodded. 'You just need to bite through this strap.' He pointed at the muzzle.

The beaver came up close to Lady, took the strap in his mouth and bit down hard with his sharp teeth. The muzzle came off and Lady shook her head in delight.

The beaver slipped the muzzle over his own head and attached the lead to the branch. Then he began pulling it towards the stream.

'Hey!' he shouted happily as Lady and Tramp trotted away. 'It works well.'

Chapter Six

'And then when she bought that muzzle for me,' Lady told Tramp, as they crossed the street, 'I got really scared.'

'That's what comes of tying yourself down to one family,' he said.

'Haven't you got a family?' Lady asked.

Tramp shook his head. 'Come on. It's supper time.'

Lady followed Tramp down the street to Tony's Restaurant. They slipped down the alley at the side and Tramp scratched at the back door. Tony – a big, jolly man – came to see who was there. When he spotted Tramp, his face lit up.

'Where've you been?' he asked. 'Hey, Joe, bring some bones.'

Lady and Tramp ate their supper and then they wandered into the park. They walked across the river in the moonlight, watching the swans gliding over the water. Then they climbed to the top of a hill and lay down to sleep.

The sound of a rooster crowing woke them up early the next morning. The sun was streaming down as Lady opened her eyes.

'Oh!' she gasped, blinking. 'Oh dear!'

'Is something wrong, pigeon?' Tramp yawned.

'It's morning,' Lady said in dismay. She jumped to her feet. 'I should have been home hours ago.'

'Why?' Tramp asked. 'Open your eyes, pigeon!'

'Open my eyes?' Lady looked puzzled.

'To what a dog's life can really be,' Tramp said impatiently. 'I'll show you what I mean.' He led Lady to the edge of the hill. 'Look down there and tell me what you see.'

Lady stared at the village below them. 'I see nice homes with gardens and fences,' she replied.

'Exactly,' Tramp snorted. 'Life on a leash! Look again, pigeon.'

This time Lady looked beyond the village, at the mountains and fields.

Tramp nodded his head. 'There's a great big hunk of world out there,' he pointed out. 'A place where two dogs can find adventure and excitement.'

'It sounds wonderful,' Lady said slowly.

'But?' Tramp added.

'But who'd watch over the baby?' asked Lady.

Tramp knew when he was beaten. 'OK, you win,' he said sadly. 'Come on, I'll take you home.'

They trotted slowly down the hill side by side, back through the park and along the alley. The dog-catcher's wagon passed by, casting a shadow over them, but

Tramp and Lady were too deep in their own thoughts to notice it.

Suddenly Tramp spotted some chickens scratching around in a nearby yard. He grinned at Lady. 'Ever chase chickens?' he enquired.

'I should say not,' Lady replied, looking quite shocked.

'Then you've never lived,' Tramp replied, crawling under the fence. 'Come on!'

Lady hesitated, then followed him. Tramp flew across the yard, yapping at the hens, who squawked indignantly and flapped their feathers. Lady began to join in, but suddenly the air echoed with the sound of gunshot.

'What's that?' Lady gasped.

'That's the signal to get going!' Tramp barked.

Lady ran for the fence and wriggled out of the yard. Panting, Tramp followed her.

'Hey, this is living!' He laughed, looking around. 'Pigeon? Hey, pigeon, where are you?'

But Lady was nowhere to be seen.

Chapter Seven

Lady lay huddled in the back of the dog-catcher's wagon, feeling very lonely and scared. The dog catcher had scooped her up in his net as she emerged from the yard where she and Tramp had been chasing chickens. Lady felt miserable and wondered sadly if she would ever see Tramp again.

The wagon had arrived at its destination and Lady was nearly deafened by the sound of dogs barking mournfully in their cages. She shivered as the guard opened the door and led her into the pound.

'Put her in number four, Bill, while I check out her licence,' he told one of the other guards.

The cage opened and Lady was pushed inside. The other dogs who were in there stared at her curiously.

'Well, look, you guys,' sneered Toughy, 'a regular Miss Park Avenue!' He stared at Lady's expensive collar. 'And she's wearing the crown jewels!'

'What did you do, sweetheart?' asked Bull. 'Give the butler fleas?'

They all howled with laughter.

A long-haired white dog who was asleep in the corner woke up and glared at them. 'Lay off,' she barked. 'Can't you see the kid's scared enough?'

'We were only having a bit of fun, Peg,' grumbled Bull. 'Ah, well, there's one dog who's never been caught.'

'Tramp's given the slip to the dog catcher every time,' agreed Toughy.

Lady's ears pricked up at the mention of Tramp's name.

'That Tramp always finds a way out of a jam!' Peg laughed.

'But remember, my friends,' barked Boris, 'even Tramp has his weakness.'

'Oh yes,' chuckled Toughy. 'The ladies!'

Lady began to look rather annoyed as the dogs started listing Tramp's girlfriends. Lulu, Trixie, Fifi, Rosita … The list went on and on. Lady was relieved when the guard came back to the cage and took her out.

'All right, baby,' he said gently to Lady. 'Someone's come to take you home.'

Jock and Trusty hurried into the garden, where Lady was lying in her kennel, her head on her paws.

'Please go away. I don't want to see anyone,' she whimpered.

It had been Aunt Sarah who had arrived at the pound to collect Lady and she'd scolded her all the way home. Now Lady had to spend the days chained up in her kennel. She wasn't allowed inside the house at all.

Before Jock and Trusty could say anything, another voice broke in.

'Hey, pigeon!'

Tramp trotted into the garden and dropped a bone at Lady's feet. 'A little something I picked up for you.' He grinned.

Lady put her nose in the air and turned her back on Tramp. Jock and Trusty ignored him too and walked off.

'Looks like I'm the one in the doghouse,' Tramp muttered. 'It wasn't my fault, pigeon –'

Lady whipped round and glared at him. 'Who's Trixie?' she demanded. 'And Lulu, Fifi and Rosita?'

Tramp looked embarrassed. 'I can explain –' he began.

'Goodbye!' Lady snapped. 'And take this with you!' She kicked the bone towards Tramp and stalked into the kennel.

Tramp padded away, looking downtrodden. Meanwhile, inside the kennel, Lady began to sob. And outside rain started to fall and lightning flashed.

Suddenly Lady lifted her head. She had spotted the glitter of dark eyes in the woodpile. The next moment the rat popped out and ran towards the house. Lady flung herself towards him, barking loudly, but was pulled back by the chain.

The rat scurried over to the trellis fixed on to the side of the house. Swiftly, he began to climb up to the open window of the nursery, where the baby slept.

Chapter Eight

Lady barked and barked as the rat climbed higher. Frantically, she pulled at the chain, trying to get free, but she couldn't.

'Stop that!' Aunt Sarah leaned out of the window and yelled at Lady.

But Lady wouldn't be quiet. Somehow she had to protect the baby. She howled helplessly as she watched the rat climb through the window into the room.

'What is it, pigeon?' Suddenly Tramp

was at Lady's side.

'A rat!' Lady gasped. 'Upstairs, in the baby's room!'

'How do I get in?' Tramp asked urgently.

'The little door on the porch,' panted Lady.

Tramp didn't waste any more time. He rushed over to Lady's dog door and flew through it. Lightning flashed as he raced quietly up the stairs towards the nursery. The room was dark, but another flash of lightning revealed the rat at the foot of the baby's cradle.

Tramp sprang forward just as the rat leapt to attack him. They fought fiercely, chasing each other round and round the cradle. Outside Lady kept on barking, tugging hard at the chain holding her back.

Suddenly the chain broke and Lady dashed across the garden. She pushed her way through the dog door and raced up the stairs. She was full of fear for the baby and worried about Tramp.

Upstairs the rat had got away from Tramp and had jumped up on to the cradle. As Lady reached the open door, the scruffy dog jumped up at the rat, knocking the cradle over. The baby began to wail loudly and Lady rushed anxiously over to him. The rat ran off across the room, but Tramp caught him behind the curtain and, a few seconds later, the rat lay still on the floor.

At that moment the light was snapped

on and Aunt Sarah rushed in. 'Oh, you poor little darling,' she gasped when she saw the overturned cradle. She turned on the dogs. 'You vicious brutes!' she snapped furiously. 'I'll call the pound!' Grabbing a broom, she drove Tramp into a nearby cupboard and slammed the door on him, as Lady watched in horror.

There was nothing Lady could do. Clutching the chain, Aunt Sarah dragged the barking spaniel down to the cellar and locked her in. Lady flung herself at the door, scratching at it in a frenzy as she heard Aunt Sarah pick up the phone and tell the dog catcher to come as quickly as he could.

Chapter Nine

Jim Dear and Darling were on their way home. As they walked down the street towards their house, they were puzzled to see the dog-catcher's wagon outside. The dog catcher was leading a big grey mongrel out of their garden.

'And if you want my advice, you'll destroy that animal at once,' called Aunt Sarah, who was standing in the doorway.

'Say, what's going on here?' Jim asked the dog catcher.

'We've been after this one for months,' the dog catcher replied. 'Caught him attacking a baby.'

'A baby!' gasped Jim and Darling.

Jock and Trusty sat watching as Jim and Darling dashed towards the house and the dog catcher drove Tramp off in his wagon.

'I was certain he was no good the moment I laid eyes on him,' Jock said sternly.

'But I never thought he'd do a thing like that,' Trusty added.

Inside the house, Aunt Sarah was explaining what had happened, while Darling held her baby tightly. 'Thank goodness I got there in time! There they were, the cradle overturned –'

Jim was frowning. 'There must be some mistake,' he said, going over to the cellar door. 'Lady wouldn't do that ...'

When he opened the door, Lady rushed out and flung herself at him. She ran over to the stairs, barking loudly.

'Watch out!' Aunt Sarah called nervously.

'She's trying to tell us something,' Jim retorted.

He followed Lady up the stairs and into the nursery. Lady pulled aside the curtain and there lay the dead rat.

'Ah!' shrieked Aunt Sarah, who had come to join them. 'A rat!'

Jock and Trusty, who were sitting by the open front door, looked at each other.

'A rat!' Trusty repeated.

'We misjudged him badly,' Jock said, shaking his head.

'Come on!' Trusty leapt to his feet. 'We've got to stop that wagon!'

He ran off down the rainy street with Jock at his heels. At the crossroads the bloodhound stopped and began sniffing the ground.

'Now what?' Jock asked. 'We both know you've lost your sense of smell!'

Trusty glared at him and carried on sniffing. Then he stiffened and raced off. Jock followed him and there, in the distance ahead of them, was the dog-catcher's wagon. The two dogs ran as fast as they could and managed to overtake it.

'Get out of the way,' the dog catcher shouted, as Jock and Trusty rushed in and out of the horses' legs.

Meanwhile, Jim and Lady were following in a taxi. Suddenly they saw the wagon ahead of them, lying on its side in the road.

Trusty was trapped beneath one of the wheels. His eyes were closed and he wasn't moving at all. Beside him Jock sat and howled mournfully.

Chapter Ten

'All right, everybody,' called Jim.
'Watch the birdie!'

It was Christmas. The candles burned
brightly on the Christmas tree and the
decorations sparkled in the firelight.
Tramp, wearing a handsome new collar,
sat up proudly to have his picture taken,
but the baby started waving a rattle in his
face. Then a puppy who looked exactly
like Tramp grabbed the baby's romper
suit in his mouth and began tugging at it.

Lady hurried over, picked up her puppy firmly in her mouth and popped him back in the box with his three sisters. All of the girls looked exactly like Lady.

'Steady now,' said Jim, pointing the camera at Tramp, Lady, the puppies and the baby. At last he took the picture, just as the visitors arrived.

'It's Jock and Trusty,' Jim called, as the two dogs made their way slowly towards the front door. Trusty had his foot bandaged and was sliding around on the snowy path.

'Merry Christmas,' Jim called from the doorway. 'Come in and I'll see about some refreshments. Darling, where did you put the dog biscuits? You know, the box Aunt Sarah sent for Christmas?'

'In the kitchen, Jim, dear,' Darling replied.

Trusty limped forward to examine Lady's puppies. 'They've got their mother's eyes,' he exclaimed.

The little boy puppy bounced up to Jock and began tugging at his tartan coat. 'But there's a bit of their father in them too!' The Scottie laughed. He looked at Tramp. 'I see you've finally got a collar.'

'Oh yes,' Tramp replied. 'And a licence.'

Outside, snow was falling softly and there was the sound of carol singing: 'All the world is calm and peaceful, all the world is bright and joyful.'

Tramp drew closer to Lady and they

smiled at each other, feeling that life couldn't be more perfect.